Dear Parents,

Welcome to the Scholastic Reader series. We have taken over 80 years of experience with teachers, parents, and children and put it into a program that is designed to match your child's interests and skills.

Level 1—Short sentences and stories made up of words kids can sound out using their phonics skills and words that are important to remember.

Level 2—Longer sentences and stories with words kids need to know and new "big" words that they will want to know.

Level 3—From sentences to paragraphs to longer stories, these books have large "chunks" of texts and are made up of a rich vocabulary.

Level 4—First chapter books with more words and fewer pictures.

It is important that children learn to read well enough to succeed in school and beyond. Here are ideas for reading this book with your child:

- Look at the book together. Encourage your child to read the title and make a prediction about the story.
- Read the book together. Encourage your child to sound out words when appropriate. When your child struggles, you can help by providing the word.
- Encourage your child to retell the story. This is a great way to check for comprehension.
- Have your child take the fluency test on the last page to check progress.

Scholastic Readers are designed to support your child's efforts to learn how to read at every age and every stage. Enjoy helping your child learn to read and love to read.

—Francie Alexander
Chief Education Officer
Scholastic Education

For my #1 Fluffy Consultant, Abraham Axler,
and his classmates,
and his teacher, Ms. Davis, at P.S. 87.
—K.M.

To Dad, who knew a good apple when he saw one.
—M.S.

Text copyright © 2001 by Kate McMullan.
Illustrations copyright © 2001 by Mavis Smith.
Activities copyright © 2003 Scholastic Inc.
All rights reserved. Published by Scholastic Inc.
SCHOLASTIC, CARTWHEEL BOOKS, FLUFFY THE CLASSROOM GUINEA PIG,
and associated logos are trademarks and/or registered trademarks of Scholastic Inc.

Library of Congress Cataloging-in-Publication Data is available.

ISBN: 0-439-31420-8

10 9 8 7   07
Printed in the U.S.A. 23 • First printing, September 2001

FLUFFY
GOES APPLE PICKING

by **Kate McMullan**

Illustrated by **Mavis Smith**

Scholastic Reader — Level 3

SCHOLASTIC INC. Cartwheel B·O·O·K·S·®

New York   Toronto   London   Auckland   Sydney
Mexico City   New Delhi   Hong Kong   Buenos Aires

I Love Apples!

School was almost over for the day.

Fluffy was napping.

"We will have a picnic tomorrow,"

Ms. Day told her class,

"when we go . . ."

"Apple picking!" everyone called.

That woke Fluffy up.

Apples? he thought. **I love apples!**

"We will go to an orchard,"
said Ms. Day. "We will see
hundreds of apple trees and
thousands of apples."
Thousands? thought Fluffy.
His eyes grew wide.
**Who knew there were THAT
many apples?**

"We will pick apples from the apple trees," said Ms. Day. "Then what will we do with some of the apples?"

"Eat them!" everyone called.

Oh, yum! thought Fluffy.

I love apples!

"Ms. Day?" said Wade.

"Can Fluffy come apple picking, too?"

Can he? thought Fluffy. **I mean, can I? Can I? PLEASE?**

"Of course, he can," said Ms. Day.

"Fluffy loves apples."

Right! thought Fluffy.

I L - O - V - E apples!

Just then, Lina from Mr. Lee's class
came through the door.
She was holding Kiss.

"Kiss's cage is a mess," said Lina.

I'll bet, thought Fluffy.

"Mr. Lee wants to give it
a good cleaning," said Lina.

"Can Kiss have a sleepover
with Fluffy tonight?"

No way! thought Fluffy.

"Sure," said Ms. Day.

Lina put Kiss into Fluffy's cage.

Kiss ran over to Fluffy's food bowl.
She started eating Fluffy's food.
Good-bye supper, thought Fluffy.
But he was too excited
about apple picking to be mad.

Kiss ate every bit of Fluffy's food.

Then she ran over to a pile of paper.

Hey! That's *my* bed, said Fluffy.

Too bad, said Kiss.

Fluffy crawled into his tube.

He was not happy

that Kiss had taken his bed.

But he was too excited

about apple picking to be mad.

Fluffy closed his eyes.
But he could not fall asleep.
For one thing, he was hungry.
And Kiss was snoring:
honk-brrrrr, honk-brrrrr.
But that's not what kept Fluffy
awake. He was too excited
about apple picking to sleep.

Fluffy tried counting apples.
One apple, two apples,
three apples, he counted.
But even that did not help.
At last the sun came up.
Fluffy had been awake all night long.
Apples! thought Fluffy.
They can wear a pig out.

Kiss Goes Apple Picking

Ms. Day and the kids came
into the classroom.
Emma and Wade
ran over to Fluffy's cage.
"Fluffy doesn't look so good," said Emma.
"He looks sleepy," said Wade.

"Kiss looks wide awake," said Wade.

"Let's take her apple picking, too."

What? thought Fluffy.

"A friend for Fluffy," said Emma.

"What a good idea!"

Not really, thought Fluffy.

"Come on, sleepy Fluffy,"
said Emma.
She picked him up and
carried him to the bus.
Wade carried Kiss.

The bus drove to the orchard.
Everyone got out
and ran to the apple trees.
"Fluffy is too sleepy to pick apples,"
said Emma.
Wrong! thought Fluffy.

"You can still have fun, Fluffy,"
said Emma. "You can watch Kiss
pick apples."
You must be joking! thought Fluffy.

Kiss picked another apple.
She ate it up. Then she ate
another one. And another!
"Too bad you are too sleepy
to eat an apple, Fluffy," said Emma.
I could never be THAT sleepy,
thought Fluffy.

Wade put Kiss into a basket
of apples.
"Have all you want!" he said.
Kiss started chomping the apples.
Fluffy could not believe his eyes.
Kiss was an apple-eating machine!

Fluffy jumped out of Emma's hands.

He ran for the basket of apples.

Look out, Kiss! he thought.

Here I come!

He took a flying leap!

He banged into his food bowl.

Ow! thought Fluffy.

"Fluffy!" said Emma.

"Are you all right?"

Fluffy looked around.

He was in his cage.

He did not see any apples.

"You were dreaming," said Emma.

Fluffy heard a terrible groan.
He turned and saw Kiss.
She was lying on her back,
holding her tummy.
Ooooh, said Kiss.
Your food made me sick!

"Kiss doesn't look so good,"
said Emma.

"Maybe she ate too much," said Wade.

"I'll take her back to Mr. Lee."
Emma picked up Fluffy.

"Let's go apple picking," she said.

All right! thought Fluffy.

Let's go!

Fluffy Goes Apple Picking

Ms. Day's class rode to the orchard.

Everyone got off the bus.

Fluffy sniffed the air.

Smells like apples! he thought.

When do we eat?

"Welcome to Hill Orchard!"
a man said. "I'm Mr. Hill.
And who is this?"
he asked when he saw Fluffy.
"This is Fluffy," said Emma.
"He's one fine pig," said Mr. Hill.
That's me! thought Fluffy.

Mr. Hill picked Fluffy up
and put him on his shoulder.
"One fine pig needs
one fine apple," he said.
When? thought Fluffy.
How about now?

"Climb into the wagon," Mr. Hill
told the kids. "I will pull you
to the top of the hill with my tractor.
Apples grow best on hilltops."
Everyone climbed into the wagon.
Go, Mr. Hill! thought Fluffy.
Get me to those apples!

Mr. Hill drove past a big red barn.

"I grow Macintosh apples," he said.

"I grow Fuji apples, too. I also grow
a kind called Granny Smith."

I'll have one of each! thought Fluffy.

Mr. Hill stopped at the top of the hill.

Everyone jumped out of the wagon.

Mr. Hill passed out baskets.

"Fill these up with apples!" he said.

Hey, Mr. Hill! thought Fluffy.

**How about filling ME up
with apples?**

Mr. Hill walked around the orchard.
Fluffy rode on his shoulder.
"Eat while you pick," said Mr. Hill.
"There is nothing as good as
an apple right off the tree."
Emma bit into an apple: *CHOMP!*
**What does a pig have to do
around here to get an apple?**
thought Fluffy.

"Okay, pig," said Mr. Hill. "Your turn."

He held Fluffy up to a branch.

Fluffy grabbed an apple. He pulled.

Nothing happened.

He pulled harder.

Nothing happened.

Fluffy pulled with all his might.

All of a sudden,
Fluffy slipped out of Mr. Hill's hand.
"Oops!" said Mr. Hill.
The branch snapped back fast,
and the apple went flying.
So did Fluffy.
AAAAAHHHHHHH!!!! thought Fluffy.

Fluffy landed with a *THUMP!*
Ms. Day turned and saw Fluffy
sitting in her apple basket.
"Fluffy!" she said.
"Where did *you* come from?"

I'll tell you later, thought Fluffy.
Right now, I've got an apple to eat.
He took a bite: *CHOMP!*

Mr. Hill drove everyone down the hill.

Ms. Day spread a cloth on the ground.

She passed around bread and cheese.

Mr. Hill poured apple cider.

All the kids ate the apples

that they had picked themselves.

Fluffy did, too. ***Mm-mm!*** he thought.

This is one fine picnic.

After the picnic,
everyone lined up for a picture.
"Say 'apples'!" said Mr. Hill.
"Wait!" said Emma. "I have a better
idea. Let's say, 'Fluffy'!"
Everyone yelled, "FLUFFY!"

It was one fine picture.